This book belongs to:

_____

Cinderella

Anastasia

Drizella

The Prince

Lady Tremaine

STARRING

The King

The Grand Duke

The Bluebirds

The Fairy Godmother

Gus

Jaq

This is a Parragon book
First published in 2007

Parragon
Queen Street House
4 Queen Street
Bath BA1 1HE, UK

ISBN 978-1-4054-8970-6
Printed in China

p

Once upon a time, there lived a kind and gentle girl called Cinderella. She was made to cook and clean and scrub for her cruel stepmother and her two spoiled stepsisters. She dreamed of falling in love and finding happiness.

Then one day, her dream came true! She married her prince, lived in a castle and had a wonderful life. Cinderella's stepsisters were left back at the chateau to do all the chores. They were extremely jealous of Cinderella.

One day, Anastasia saw Cinderella and the Prince riding into the forest. She followed and found that the Fairy Godmother had organized a surprise anniversary party for the happy couple.

With a wave of her wand, the Fairy Godmother changed Cinderella's and the Prince's clothes into ballroom finery.

"So that's how Cinderella did it," exclaimed Anastasia. "Magic!"

At that moment, the Fairy Godmother threw up her arms in delight, and the wand flew out of her hand. It landed next to Anastasia, who picked it up and raced home to show her mother and sister.

"Mother! Our troubles are over!" cried Anastasia, showing her the wand.

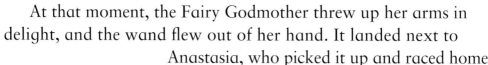

"Child, put that down," said the Fairy Godmother, who had followed Anastasia home. "In the wrong hands that wand could be extremely dangerous."

But Anastasia would not give up the wand.

"Bibbidi-bobbidi-boo!" she said, and a stream of magic accidentally turned Lucifer into something between a cat and a goose. Then she turned the Fairy Godmother into a statue!

Lady Tremaine snatched the wand from Anastasia.

"It means power…riches…revenge!" she cried. And with that she waved the wand and began to turn back time…all the way back to exactly one year earlier.

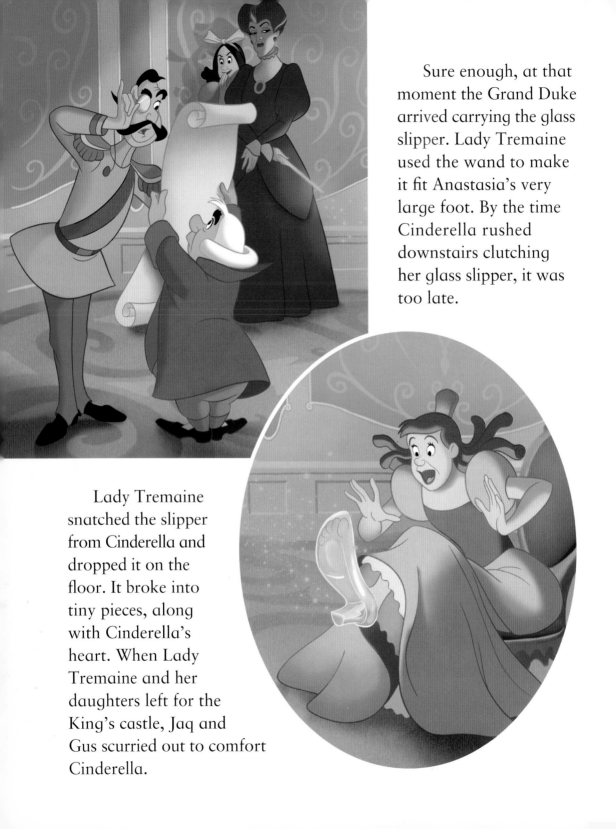

Sure enough, at that moment the Grand Duke arrived carrying the glass slipper. Lady Tremaine used the wand to make it fit Anastasia's very large foot. By the time Cinderella rushed downstairs clutching her glass slipper, it was too late.

Lady Tremaine snatched the slipper from Cinderella and dropped it on the floor. It broke into tiny pieces, along with Cinderella's heart. When Lady Tremaine and her daughters left for the King's castle, Jaq and Gus scurried out to comfort Cinderella.

Cinderella decided to go to the castle to see the Prince. She knew that when he saw her again everything would be alright. She slipped in through the servants' entrance and told the house-keeper that she was the royal mouse-catcher.

Gus and Jaq leaped out of Cinderella's pocket and scurried across the floor. The kitchen was soon in chaos and Cinderella was able to slip away to search for the Prince.

Meanwhile, Jaq and Gus hid in the royal parlour to watch the arrival of Lady Tremaine, Anastasia and Drizella.

The Prince raced in excitedly, but when he saw Anastasia wearing the glass slipper his face dropped. He knew something was wrong.

Lady Tremaine quickly waved the magic wand. Evil magic surrounded the Prince. He suddenly pulled out a ring.

"Will you marry me?" he asked Anastasia.

She quickly agreed and the ceremony was arranged for that very night.

A little while later, Cinderella found the Prince in a palace garden. The Prince did not seem to remember dancing with her at the ball. Before Cinderella had time to explain, she was called away by the house-keeper to catch the mice in the cellar.

Gus and Jaq explained to Cinderella that Lady Tremaine had used the wand to put the Prince under a spell.

"We have to get that wand," said Cinderella.

Meanwhile, Anastasia and Drizella were arguing in the banqueting hall. They were so busy throwing food at each other that they didn't notice the Prince and the King enter the room. The Prince looked at Anastasia adoringly despite her terrible behaviour. Awkwardly, he suggested a dancing lesson.

Afterwards, the King demanded to see Anastasia alone. Instead of being angry because of her clumsy dancing, he gave her a gift. It was the Queen's most prized possession – a seashell.

"When our hands touched," he told Anastasia, "I knew I had found true love."

"Just by touching her hand?" she asked.

Upstairs, Cinderella watched through a keyhole as Lady Tremaine scolded Drizella for playing with the wand. She locked it in a drawer and put the key in her pocket. Cinderella asked the bluebirds to find the Prince, while Gus and Jaq slipped into the room to get the key.

As the mice crept past Lucifer they accidentally pushed his tail into the fire. The shocked cat leaped around the room, howling. Cinderella disguised herself as a maid and rushed in to help the mice. Lady Tremaine soon recognized her, but it didn't matter – Gus and Jaq had the wand!

Lucifer chased Jaq and Gus down the stairs. Jaq zapped him with the wand and he turned Lucifer into a cat-in-the-box, but he carried on chasing the mice. Jaq used the wand again and he turned Lucifer into a very, very tiny cat!

The mice ran into a mouse hole and Lucifer followed. Jaq zapped the tiny cat again and changed him back to his normal size. Lucifer was stuck fast in the hole! The mice rushed off to give Cinderella the wand.

Gus and Jaq arrived just as the bluebirds returned with the Prince. Then Lady Tremaine appeared with the royal guards. She snatched the wand and ordered a guard to put Cinderella on the next ship leaving the kingdom. Cinderella touched the Prince's hand and pleaded with him as she was led away.

The Prince couldn't stop thinking about Cinderella. Gus and Jaq caught his attention and told him the whole story. Then the bluebirds showed him the glass slipper that they had carefully mended.

"I have to find her!" declared the Prince.

When the King heard that the Prince was leaving, he tried to stop him, but the Prince leaped out of a window and jumped on his horse. He galloped under the closing gate and set off to find Cinderella.

When the Prince arrived at the dock, the ship had already left. He sped off towards a warehouse high on the cliff. His horse was just about to jump through an opening overlooking the ocean when it froze. The Prince went flying over the reins.

Cinderella looked up to see the Prince slashing through the ship's sails with his knife. When he reached the deck, he took Cinderella by the hand.

"Remember me?" he asked.

When their hands touched, the magic they had felt at the ball came flooding back. The spell was broken.

"Will you marry me... Cinderelly?" asked the Prince, using the name Gus and Jaq had told him.

"Yes," replied Cinderella, smiling. "But actually, it's Cinderella."

The Prince and Cinderella rode back to the castle and immediately told the King about Lady Tremaine's wicked plans. The guards went to arrest them. But when they got to their room the ladies were nowhere to be found.

Lady Tremaine had used the wand to make herself, Drizella and Anastasia vanish!

"Search my entire kingdom!" commanded the King angrily. "I want them found and arrested!"

A new wedding ceremony was planned for that evening. As Cinderella dressed she had an unwelcome visit from Lady Tremaine – and another Cinderella! Lady Tremaine had used the wand to turn Anastasia into Cinderella's twin.

"The Prince won't be fooled," Cinderella told Lady Tremaine.

"The Prince will never know," she replied.

Cinderella asked Anastasia if she truly loved the Prince. But before Anastasia could answer, Lady Tremaine used the wand to make Cinderella, Gus and Jaq disappear.

When the trio reappeared they found themselves trapped inside a giant pumpkin coach. The coach driver cracked the whip – it was Lucifer, transformed by the Stepmother into a human!

The mice managed to crawl through the thorny vines that covered the windows. Gus went to unhitch the horse while Jaq distracted Lucifer, but Lucifer spotted Gus. He grabbed the brave little mouse and got ready to eat him!

Cinderella forced her way from the coach just in time. She toppled Lucifer off his seat, then Gus and Jaq disconnected the carriage. The three jumped onto the horse just in time to see the carriage fly over the cliff! They galloped off towards the castle.

But the wedding had already begun! Anastasia – transformed into Cinderella – was led down the aisle by the King. She glanced at the seashell he had given her. The Prince looked at Anastasia lovingly.

"My one and only Cinderella," he said.

Anastasia began to have second thoughts.

"Do you, Cinderella, take this man as your lawfully wedded husband?" asked the Bishop.

"Say 'I do!'" hissed Lady Tremaine from her hiding place behind a curtain.

When Anastasia touched his hand, it was clear to the Prince that this was the wrong girl.

Suddenly, the chapel doors flew open – it was the real Cinderella!

Everybody gasped. Lady Tremaine pulled out the magic wand and pointed it at Anastasia and Cinderella. The Prince jumped in front of them. The magic from the wand bounced off his sword and turned Lady Tremaine and Drizella into toads!

The Prince touched the real Cinderella's hands and knew she was the one he loved.

Anastasia changed herself back and helped Cinderella remove the spell from the Fairy Godmother – who in turn gave Cinderella brand new wedding finery.

Anastasia returned the seashell to the King. "I don't deserve this," she said.

Handing it back he said, "Everyone deserves true love."

"Well, does anyone want to marry my son?" he asked.

"I do!" answered Cinderella.

"Then I now pronounce you husband and wife," proclaimed the Bishop.

And they lived happily ever after... again.

❋ ❋ ❋